Fire at Gray Wolf Lookout

a Firehawks romance story
by
M. L. Buchman

Buchman Bookworks

1

The view of the Lolo National Forest on the Idaho-Montana border spread for a hundred miles in every direction. And Gray Wolf Summit fire lookout tower commanded one of the most beautiful and most remote regions of the forest. From his perch Tom Cunningham could see much of the Lolo, a big chunk of the Clearwater, and even the north tip of the Selway-Bitterroot Wilderness.

Despite being in his mid-twenties, he felt like the luckiest kid in the U.S. Forest Service. No one was watching, so what the heck, he spit off the edge of the tower. Like a twelve-year old, he watched as the light breeze carried it past the cliff and down into the canyon—he watched it as long as he could.

The whole acting-his-age thing had never really worked for him anyway, and someday he'd have to apologize to his parents for that. Both professors at the University of Washington—English lit Dad and Mom the chemist—and Tom had used his degree in geology to be an auto body shop mechanic.

His rut was obvious, didn't need to be on the outside to see it, Tom could feel it from the inside just fine. Like the crippled vehicles that streamed through his shop door, he couldn't seem to drive straight down any path…and that was on the rare occasions when he got running at all.

Screw that!

Last winter he'd gotten so sick of himself that he figured the best solution was to get away—way away!

He'd grown up in Seattle's Wallingford neighborhood, side-by-side housing that would be suburbia if it wasn't now tucked well inside city limits. It was also saved from that awful fate because the houses were fifty to a hundred years old rather than tract built pillboxes.

However, his experience with the great outdoors was limited to a couple of trips out to Snoqualmie Falls, a two hundred-and-fifty foot waterfall up in the Cascades. A good place for taking a girl on a nice date as the lodge had an excellent brunch.

His present situation, atop a Montana fire lookout tower, had been Lucy's idea. After six months of sharing a bed most nights she'd told him to go jump into a fire—not her exact words. Something about his total lack of either direction or ambition. Hearing this from his parents he could tune out. Hearing it from a hot brunette as he watched her fine behind departing his third-floor apartment for the last time, that was a bit harder to ignore.

He'd hopped on the Internet. And when he'd looked up fire—for lack of anything better to do—an image of wildfire had caught his attention. Somehow, that single glimpse had led to enrolling in a fire lookout certification course and quitting his job as a car mechanic.

"Now you've done it, buddy," Tom looked out at the view and decided that whether stupid, whimsical, or psychotic, it had been a damn fine decision—perhaps the first good one in his adult life.

He clamped his hands on the heavy wood rail and gave it a shake—not even a wiggle. His new home was as solid as the rock it stood on.

The Gray Wolf Summit lookout tower was perched at over seven thousand feet. The valleys fell away on three sides down to three thousand feet and then soared vertically back up, though few of the peaks reached his lofty height. To the north, the ridge descended less dramatically, giving him a long slope of hikeable terrain.

He'd never done much hiking, but couldn't wait to try it out. Per Forest Service training, he had his bear-sized can of pepper spray, supposedly the safest and most effective solution to stop a bear. Same size as a can of spray paint, it shot a cloud of pepper that was the most effective way to stop a charging bear—far better than a big gun, the numbers said. He still would have liked a big gun, but since he'd be as likely to shoot himself as the bear, he'd decided against it.

Beneath his boot soles, he stood on a planked walkway twenty-three feet above the rocky summit ridge; the true summit —a rounded crown of rock—lay fifty feet west and half as high as his tower. The forest fire lookout tower that would be his home for the next five months was a heavy wooden structure. Massive beams of rough-hewn dark wood formed the crisscross framework that supported the tower. Thirty-seven steps made of two-inch thick planks of Douglas fir led up to the fourteen-foot square glass-windowed "cab" that was now home. Those old Depression-era CCC guys really knew how to build something to last; most of the towers and lodges in the Pacific Northwest and Montana had been put up by those "back to work" crews.

He breathed in the air and held it as long as he could. He wanted to savor its taste, its clarity, the complete absence of any hint of civilization or old motor oil. He was so sick of all the people who thought their car was so darned important. It's a machine, people, use it, don't marry it. He was glad to be away from them.

He was almost as sick of them as he was of himself, which was really saying something.

The true extent of his aloneness he was less comfortable with.

Tom's next nearest neighbors were Tess and Jack on Cougar Peak lookout fifteen miles to the north, Swallow Hill twenty miles to the southwest, and—according to his radio plan—Old Crag equally far to the east.

Gray Wolf Summit wasn't on some through-trail, or a trail to anywhere at all except Gray Wolf Summit. It had been a long eight-mile hike with a gargantuan pack that had him cursing in the first mile as he crested a thousand-foot climb only to descend into an even deeper valley.

Vic, the Forest Service ranger in charge of the Selway-Bitterroot and Lolo lookouts, had warned him that his likely visitors over the summer would be the mule skinner who delivered the bulk of his supplies, his substitute who would come up for two days out of every two weeks, and one or two extreme fire-lookout tourists. Gray Wolf, perched at the end of a dead-end trail, was a brutal enough hike to discourage all except the most dedicated.

"Well," he told a turkey buzzard soaring on the high winds with its wing-tip feathers spread like fingers—the bird was probably the only one he'd be talking to most of the time. "If you're seeking something that died, you can cart off the Old Me."

He didn't know who he'd be by the end of the summer, that's why he was up here. But he knew he wasn't going to be the wandering soul who was presently standing on the lookout tower.

It was going to be an interesting summer.

2

Patty Dale hiked up the narrow trail. She'd been looking forward to this summer for four years now. Sure, it was the ass end of wildlife biology—first-year field work—but she didn't care. Being paid to tramp over the mountains and valleys of the Lolo for the next year was her idea of heaven.

She'd absolutely paid her dues.

"No one," her parents had told her, "no one does Army ROTC as a wildlife biologist." Her fellow cadets agreed, but she'd known what she wanted to do since the first reintroduced wolves were released into

Yellowstone Park on her sixth birthday
—March 21, 1995 after a seventy-year
absence.

"Just watch me," though she'd said it
only to herself at the time.

Now, after four years in the Army, she'd
have said aloud, "Who the fuck do you
think you are, judging my ass?"

Patty liked the self-confidence she'd
learned in the military, though she was
going to have to clean up her language—
another gift of her military service—now
that she was an academic, working for the
Montana Fish, Wildlife & Parks.

An academic—first in her family past
high school. First not to work in the
open-pit copper mines of Butte, Montana.
Busted flat when the operations closed
down for several years in the '80s and again
when she was in her teens. She was the only
one to make it out.

Now, at twenty-six she'd done her time
and survived her two full tours overseas.
For the rest of her life, she would get to
do what *she* wanted to. And right now that
included hunting gray wolves—the largest

of the wild canines—with a camera and a notebook.

It seemed cliché, but two wolf packs had bred in dens on the mid-level slopes to either side of Gray Wolf Summit. The chance to study two packs simultaneously was almost unheard of. Her rookie year was going to fucking rock…to seriously rock. Whatever.

Patty would be spending most of her time down in the forest, but the chance to sit on Gray Wolf Summit before she did was too perfect to pass up.

Shaded north sections of the trail were still covered with snow. Typical June in Montana. Portions of the mountains were still thick with winter, while in other sections the aspen and maple leafed out in a hundred shades of bright green. The dark spruce and Douglas fir grew bright fingertips at the end of every branch making the mountainside glow with new life.

She took her time hiking up the trail. Rabbit pellets and deer scat littered the trail here and there. Wolf tracks crossed the trail in a section just a half-mile long, this is where she'd start tomorrow. A single massive bear's paw print, in the mud close beside a racing stream of snowmelt runoff, was the first she'd ever seen on her own. She took a photo of it next to her own size six hiking boot. It would look great on her wall, if she ever got a place of her own.

Right now, home was a barracks in Helena, two hundred miles to the east. She didn't plan on being there much this year.

She filled her water bottles, dropped a purification tablet and an electrolyte packet into each one, resettled her pack, and continued up the trail.

Patty made it to the peak after full dark. The fire lookout tower was a blacked-out silhouette against the stars. She dropped her pack and sighed, glad to be free of the load. Using only the starlight, she rolled out an air mattress on the lichen and climbed into her sleeping bag on the very summit. She lay awake a long time after finishing an energy bar and an apple for dinner. Her contentment reached far and wide, watching her breath turn to mist before dissipating against a wilderness of stars.

She knew a lot of the constellations, but the old stories never seemed to fit. Well, now they had plenty of time to become friends. She had been planning to pick up a book, or at least one of those charts with the pretty drawings so that she'd really know the constellations by summer's end. Then she decided that she'd rather make up her own mythology, reinvent herself in the here and now.

She'd never really seen the big bear of Ursa Major in the Big Dipper. It was just a dipper. From now on, it would be dedicated to her first drink of stream water now that she was free.

Hercules was high in the sky, a wasp-waisted group of stars with a sword raised high. She renamed it Warrior Patty. Four years she'd fought for the U.S. Army. Before that she'd fought against the vortex of her family's history that had threatened to suck her down into the copper mine as well.

She fell asleep before she'd decided how to rename Cygnus the Swan flying up over the eastern horizon.

3

Tom woke in his lookout "cab" disoriented by the soft dawn light in such a foreign place. His body felt like he'd been battered by the night. The silence was so deep that his ears had rung loud enough to keep him awake. And no matter how deeply he tucked into his sleeping bag, he couldn't seem to get away from the cold.

And there had been the noises.

With the sunset, the world had gone silent, every bird asleep, his buddy the buzzard nesting somewhere in the trees far below. Not a breath of wind.

Then, he'd heard animals rustle about outside and imagined the worst. After a loud thump and strange, soft call like a sigh, there had been slick, snake-like sounds he couldn't identify. Torn between cold and fear, he'd decided that getting up to lock his front door situated at the top of thirty-seven stairs really wasn't necessary—not if he wanted to have any self-respect in the morning.

On the verge of getting up to lock it anyway, a wolf howl lifted into the night. He pictured a entire pack storming his tower if he made the slightest noise. The single cry was far off and left him awake and shivering for hours.

With large windows encircling his cabin in the sky—his tiny summer home was almost entirely glass from waist to head-high—the low sunlight was rapidly heating it up from sub-Arctic to toasty. Around the edges it had a bed, desk, two comfortable chairs, and a long worktable with a pair of stools facing an amazing view. The entire view was amazing. He could see no signs of civilization in any direction and he was above the whole forest.

Up above the wrap-around windows was an outlined drawing that was a map of the surrounding terrain which named every peak and valley for three-hundred-and-sixty degrees. In the center stood a raised cabinet topped by the Osborne Fire Finder for locating a burn if he saw one.

The first thing Tom did after crawling out of his sleeping bag was to pick up the big binoculars and scan the horizon and the trees for smoke. His training had made sure he remembered to look both near and far—to scan the nearby slopes as well as the distant peaks. The fire season didn't officially start for a few days and he knew that it could be weeks before he saw his first one, if he saw one at all.

Three-quarters of the way around, he yelped.

Smoke!

A huge plume of it.

Still holding the binoculars, he waved his other hand around reaching for his radio when he caught a view of something silver.

Tom peeked over the top of the binoculars, but couldn't see any fire down toward Cougar Peak or in the valley directly below.

But the thing had been massive.

And then he looked closer.

A woman with light-colored hair was sitting cross-legged in front of a small fire that occasionally released a little puff of smoke. The flash of silver was a small cooking pot. Even as he watched, she tipped it into a mug and then dumped in a slim packet of—he adjusted the binoculars' focus—instant coffee.

He swung the glasses up to see her face…and she was looking right at him.

Okay, voyeuristic. He lowered the glasses and waved before it could become voyeuristic in a bad way. She didn't wave back.

He stepped out the door onto the walkway around the cab.

"Sorry," he called out. "I thought you were a forest fire."

"Well, that's a new one."

At just fifty feet away he could see she sat on a heavy field pack. She wore a thick jacket, messy light-brown hair ruffled down to her collar. Looking at her all wrapped up, he suddenly realized he was freezing his balls off. He looked down.

Briefs and binoculars.

"Holy crap!" he hurried back inside to the sound of her snort of amusement.

4

About the time Patty finished making her oatmeal in the same pot she'd made coffee, the lookout guy emerged again. This time he was wearing enough layers to look like the Michelin tire man.

Too bad. He'd looked good in just his tighty-whities. He wasn't macho-soldier strong, but he was close.

She'd done her best not to think about men since she'd gotten her commander court-martialed for thinking he could take liberties. It had led to her complete isolation by the men in the unit, and by the women as well—a lot of whom were screwing other soldiers, married and not. Totally gross.

Mr. Fire Lookout stood about six feet and didn't move down the stairs like an athlete or a soldier. He moved like a geek. Even though he now carried a mug of his own, he didn't approach her campfire until she waved him over.

Man unsure of himself. That was a new one. Most guys, especially the ones without a clue, moved with a self-entitled assuredness and bravado that only served to piss her off.

He moved close to the fire but didn't sit, instead looming above her. Well, she wasn't going to crick her neck for any male of the species.

"Sit down or shove off," she pulled out a squeeze bottle of maple syrup and drizzled a scant teaspoon on her oatmeal to make the syrup last.

"Sorry," he sat. So not a total write-off.

Patty hadn't really wanted company, but then again, she was the one who'd camped by a lookout tower—you get what you pay for. "Got a name?"

"Yes. Do you?"

She almost spewed her first mouthful of scalding oatmeal in his face along with her barely contained laughter.

Handsome unsure guy with a sense of humor?

"Sure," she kept eating and they shared a smile. "They're useful things to have…at times. I'll just call you Fireboy."

"Works for me." Still he didn't ask her name and she could no longer conveniently ask for his. Instead he sipped his coffee and stared out at the sunlight-etched shadows as sunrise moved across the tree-dark slopes.

This was why she'd come here, to watch daybreak sweep over the rugged mountains.

It certainly wasn't to be studying the profile of the man etched against the softening blue sky.

5

Tom stared into the distance and struggled for something to say. Though women didn't make him tongue-tied, he knew that he wasn't the smoothest guy around. Now Jimmy at the auto-body shop could talk female clients out of their BMWs and straight into a hotel room, but Tom had never figured out how.

But after convincing himself that he was alone in the wilderness, then flashing himself at a woman camping at the edge of a thousand foot drop-off, he didn't know what to say. She was pretty, at least her face and hair were. Her fingers were fine and strong. The rest of her was covered in a thick jacket, many-pocketed camo pants, and heavy hiking boots.

The women he knew were the sorts who wanted to hit a movie or go out drinking. Outdoorsy ones would play Frisbee on the lawn at Gasworks Park overlooking Lake Union and downtown Seattle.

This one was sitting on a pack that looked heavier than his had been and was cooking breakfast over an open campfire a dozen miles from the next nearest living soul.

"What brings you to Gray Wolf Summit?" That was safe enough, wasn't it?

"Exactly," she mumbled as she sucked in cool pine air over a hot mouthful of oatmeal. She didn't elaborate.

"You came for the summit?"

"No, the gray wolf part."

Was she naturally prickly or was she just teasing him? He decided to wait her out. After all, he'd felt plenty lonely last night— not knowing that an attractive woman was camped just a shout away—and it was only his first day in the wilderness. He didn't want to scare off what might be his only visitor for the entire summer.

"Wildlife biologist. I'm here to monitor the gray wolf dens off either side of the trail," she hooked a thumb back over her shoulder.

"They're here?" He spun to look, feeling as if one was about to attack him from behind. Nothing but the rolling line of the ridge, the narrow alpine meadow of grass and wildflowers with his wooden outhouse perched a few hundred feet downslope. Beyond that, the short scrub trees that eked out a living high on the granite, though their spareness quickly developed into a thick forest.

"Sure," she said, continuing to pay attention to her oatmeal and the distant mountains. "Plenty of trail sign if you'd known what to look for on your way up."

He could hear all of the points he'd just lost by missing the "shit signs." Like how was he supposed to know. Though drawings did fill the tiny safety handbook the Forest Service had given him during training.

"There are two known dens and we think they're both occupied. I'm going to watch, record, set camera traps…all of the fun stuff." She'd finished off her breakfast and returned to her coffee.

"You don't look like a lunatic."

"Don't ask my former commander."

"Deal." Ex-military, which made the "lunatic" assessment even less likely. This was a woman with skills and a lack of fear because of those skills.

Whereas he had a complete lack of wilderness skills, which totally explained last night. Well, he wouldn't be letting himself go there again. From now on his fears would only be real ones.

"I'll just call you Wolfgirl."

"You're saying I'm not a woman?" No sense of offense, as if she was just asking.

"Wolfwoman doesn't exactly trip off the tongue. Besides, if I'm Fireboy, you're stuck with Wolfgirl."

"As long as you aren't calling me a bitch."

Female wolf. Bitch. "Don't know you well enough to decide one way or another."

"I'll be around. By the end of the summer, you'll know for sure that I am."

She'd be around.

He'd spent much of last night wondering if there was any way he could cut and run. Fire tower, isolation, howling wolves, the whole bit. Now, no more imaginary fears and, maybe, he wouldn't be so alone all summer.

A regular visitor.

He could deal with that.

6

Tom had settled into a semblance of
routine after the first couple weeks. Up
with the sun—he'd never been an early
riser—but there wasn't much to do up
here at night except watch the stars. First
scan of the horizon for the day, then a
couple-hour hike up and down the trail.
Eventually, he'd branched off the trail for
longer and longer forays through the pine
and fir forest. He started seeing the "shit
signs" but decided that unless they were
still steaming he wasn't going to worry, too
much. The one time he saw bear scat—

freaking gigantic—he actually pulled his pepper spray can from his hip holster for the rest of that hike.

At first, he'd been hoping to run into Wolfgirl, but then he'd started noticing the wildlife and the plants changed with elevation along the trail. The Forest Service safety guide let him identify the basics, but he'd get a better guidebook on his first break back in town.

He was on duty from nine a.m. til six in the evening. He sent a morning radio report of weather readings and the fact that he was "in service." Every fifteen minutes, scan the horizon for "a smoke"—the little wisp of white that promised fire close behind. It was a little dizzying at times sweeping the binoculars up and down the hills—they went on forever. Once he got disoriented enough he couldn't remember where he'd started and had to go around a second time. After that he started and ended with due north.

Due north was the trail that Wolfgirl had walked down two weeks ago, swinging her monstrous backpack on as if it weighed nothing at all.

He felt better when he noticed that she too carried the bear spray rather than a gun. She was a wildlife biologist, so he'd guess that she knew what was best. And being a soldier meant that she had a handgun skill set that he didn't.

When she'd stood up, she'd been smaller than he'd expected. Somehow a person who tracked over the wilderness fearlessly seeking a massive four-legged predator should stand more than five-foot six. His final view of her had been a single pair of slender, camo-clad legs sticking out from below her pack and a battered blue baseball cap with a Montana State University bobcat logo above.

After two weeks—and still no sign of Wolfgirl—he'd had his first two days "down." A lookout relief had hiked in and continued the firewatch while he got off the mountain and went into town—a four-hour hike out and another hour skidding his car down muddy logging roads and then the bland pavement of the highway to Missoula. A night at the bar and crashing in a cheap motel. Alone.

There'd been a couple of potentials at the bar, but he wasn't into it. He'd had his fair share of cheap sex—it usually cost a couple beers, some nachos, and a little dancing. It had always bothered him that the dancing was often better than the cheap sex.

He hadn't felt that way at first, of course. Women in bars had started happening for him as he'd shifted from geeky academic to muscled mechanic from wrenching on crumpled car frames all day. It was true, macho guys got the hot women and he'd certainly enjoyed the benefits of that at first. But now, his ego didn't need the boost and he just didn't care for the hollow feeling morning-afters always left.

Technically, he had another day down. Instead, he hit the bookstore for a wilderness guide. *Flora and Fauna of the Lolo Forest* was perfect. Then he spotted a title on wolves and grabbed it too. It had become clear that Wolfgirl was gone from his life, but he wanted to read up on them anyway. Tom went through the grocery store, loaded up his pack to a ridiculous weight, and struggled back up to the summit.

And Wolfgirl had left him a note with the substitute lookout.

Hi! and a line-drawing of what he now recognized as a wolf's paw print for a signature. Later that afternoon, he'd been idly doodling between lookout duties, and had drawn wind-blown hair around the paw print as if it was a face.

He didn't know why it mattered, but it did.

Shit!

7

It was late afternoon and Patty should
have headed down the trail and into town.
She hated to be away from the mountain
and her wolf dens. There were two packs.
One pack of six had a dozen pups just
starting to peek their noses out of the
dens. The other was a threesome led by a
great, black-furred male; the smaller pack
had just five pups as far as she could tell.
The two groups had very little to do with
each other except for the older female of
the threesome, gray in the muzzle, who
hunted across the range. It was her tracks

that crossed the trail back and forth. All the other wolves hunted down the valleys on their own sides of the ridge.

Patty had spent three intense weeks trying to track that lone female and discover what she was doing on both sides, but hadn't found out yet. Patty monitored the packs nonstop, except for an afternoon, going up to the lookout tower, only to discover that was Fireboy's day off the mountain.

Quite what had drawn her up the mountain that day was unclear. She'd only shared a cup of coffee and a few jokes, but he'd stuck in her mind. One thing she'd learned in the Army was to pay attention to those little things. In Iraq, wondering about that unexplained cardboard box along the roadside, could be someone's groceries, could be an IED. Don't remember that pile of cut wheat stalks off the side of the road at the junction? Turns out to be perfect cover for a shooter.

Now she was back again, to find out what had stuck in her mind about Fireboy. She thought about kicking the timber at ground-level a couple of times to announce she was coming. Then she remembered his seriously cute, "Holy crap!" when he'd discovered he wasn't wearing anything but very tight briefs and binoculars.

Patty kept her gait light on the stairs and moved upward silently despite her heavy pack which had become like a second skin. On the way up, she could only marvel at the view after having her head down in the woods for three weeks. She so loved being out here.

Up at the catwalk level, she could see through the broad windows into the cabin—it was a very fine view indeed. He was wearing shorts, but that was all. It was June 21st according to her observations log book, mid-summer's eve, and the late afternoon sun was warm.

The stairs had landed her at the north side, close beside the door. Fireboy was facing away from her doing a slow methodical scan of the hills to the south. Now only ten feet away, she could see the definition of his shoulder muscles put on display by his raised arms.

Clean, no tats, like a canvas not yet written upon. Beneath her shirt she wore a lone she-wolf face on her left shoulder blade. Eyes closed, howling a song of purest joy.

He slowly turned in her direction as he inspected his way around the hills. The abs definition from the side was just as nice.

Then facing her…and finally the fat end of the binocs lined up on her face and she smiled.

"Holy crap!" just like the first time. He jerked down the glasses and looked at her blankly.

She didn't know what response she wanted or expected from him. But it was a good one when it came—

"Wolfgirl!" His smile was huge and welcoming. Then he raised the binoculars again and got points for not aiming them at her breasts. "My, what big teeth you have."

Patty laughed. It was something she hadn't done in a long time. Not since before her commander had almost succeeded in raping her—"because deep down she really wanted it"—before she succeeded in breaking his face—"because deep down he really wanted it." Not since…she didn't know when.

8

Tom was glad it was the end of the afternoon watch, his last scan of the peaks and valleys for the day. She was actually here, standing in his doorway as if that was somehow completely normal. Only habit reminded him to call in an end-of-day report of "no smokes, no fire activity, Gray Wolf Summit out of service."

He thought about all of the clichés. "You're here!" "Wasn't expecting you!" Really wasn't.

He also hadn't known quite how beautiful she was. He'd seen her face before, clear skin, dark eyes of unfathomable depth. Even in the three weeks since he'd last seen her, her hair had grown and now looked just a little out of control, a touch wild. She was what the guys at the shop would have called a "solid gal." Not heavy—there was not an ounce of heavy anywhere on Wolfgirl—but not slender or model frail either. She was the kind of woman who had the strength to do something other than look good in clothes. The chest and waist belts of her pack stretched her thin cotton t-shirt tight over her breasts. Very nice.

Say something you idiot!

"Was that you I heard howling at the moon last night?"

"Might have," that grin lit up her face even brighter.

Forget pretty, plug in gorgeous with that smile.

"Catch any fires yet?" she asked.

He slapped a hand tragically to his chest, and realized that once again he was mostly unclothed in front of her. *Go with it.* "Not so much as a firefly," he moaned like a player in a Shakespearean drama.

"Not much of a Fireboy, are you?"

He tried to sigh tragically.

Must have worked; that surprising, musical laugh reemerged.

"How goes the wolf hunt?" he wanted to keep her talking.

"Fucking awesome!"

"Drop your pack…" *please stay awhile,* "…and tell me."

She did, dropping it with a heavy thunk that seemed to shake the cab with its weight. She pulled out a water bottle and turned to point north.

Then she cursed, "Do you have a map?"

Now it was his turn to laugh. There was the drawing around the whole top of the wall. There was the wide area map mounted on the Osborne finder that gave him the area for fifty miles in every direction. And on the main desk he kept a 7-1/2-minute quadrangle map rolled out. It showed the area for seven-and-a-half miles north of Cougar Peak—the area he'd known she was tramping.

"Do you have the fifteen?"

He pulled out the larger area 15-minute map.

For the next half hour she led him on a tour of a vast range of hills and valleys, amazing him with the amount of territory she and the wolves covered. Her hard-bitten nails tracing the lines of brutal climbs that had nothing to do with fire-tower trails or logging roads. She'd been hiking straight through brush. The excitement in her voice was so true and pure and it evoked a whole series of emotions.

At first, awe that anyone could care so much about…anything. She was pulling out her log book to trace the wolves' movements more accurately over the terrain of the map.

Then it was discomfort and finally a shame that had him shuffling foot to foot. He cared about nothing this much; the past few years he'd mostly felt…just blank.

What the hell was he doing with his life?

A college degree he couldn't imagine ever using, a career that included wiping blood, vomit, and empty beer bottles out of shattered cars before he could even work on them, and now sitting alone watching a forest that might never catch on fire. Even if it did, the more experienced spotters at Cougar Peak or Old Crag would probably spot it long before he did.

But finally Wolfgirl overwhelmed his sense of uselessness. Her excitement swept him aboard.

When she spotted Dutcher and Dutcher's *The Hidden Life of Wolves* on his desk, she cried for joy and dragged it onto the map to flip pages searching for pictures that would show him what The Messenger—as she'd dubbed the traveling female—looked like. He'd barely been able to focus on the pictures as they rubbed shoulders and jostled together hip to hip while she told more stories.

He'd made dinner, that she'd bolted, and they'd made love on his narrow bunk as the sunset filled the fire tower with the colors of fire. She rose over him, feral, powerful, as wild as her wolves. The red-gold light played over her skin as she threw her head back and cried out when he sheathed himself and entered her.

Tom half expected her to howl, instead she groaned like her heart had been ripped from her chest. He leaned up to bury his lips and his face between her breasts and she pulled him in with a truth, with an honesty of emotion he'd never found in a woman before.

This was not a woman who revved his engines or fit him like the seat of a Porsche 944 Turbo. She was too primal, too purely herself for that.

When their climaxes ripped through them he felt every jolt through her body as if it was his own.

And after their pulses peaked then slowed and their bodies both shuddered until she finally lay still upon his chest, then she wept.

He held her, stroked her hair, and whispered in her ear that she was okay.

Okay? She was life-changing amazing, but that wasn't what she needed to hear right now as the sobs wracked her, as the smell of salt tears washing against his cheek threatened to overpower the scent of the forest that clung to her hair.

They slept clinging tightly to each other.

In the middle of the night, she woke him, and by the light of the stars she lay beneath him and they were as gentle with each other as they'd been frantic earlier.

Tom woke alone with the sunlight streaming over him.

A note rested on the open page of *The Hidden Lives of Wolves*.

> *I owe you three pounds of oatmeal,*
> *a half bottle of maple syrup,*
> *and a box of energy bars.*
> *You're very pretty when you sleep.*

Again, the paw-print signature.

This time there was a radio frequency.

She'd left the note on the picture of the wolf he'd chosen as prettiest in the whole book. It was a close-up of a black-furred wolf. Just her face, with her chin resting on the snow, yellow eyes looking right at the camera.

9

Patty went back to him whenever she could tear herself away.

Talked to him by radio on other nights when he wasn't on fire watch and the wolves weren't on an active hunt.

June passed into July.

Fireboy's first fire sighting had them talking for hours over their radios. She normally limited herself to fifteen minutes to conserve batteries, but he'd been so excited she couldn't help herself and let him roll. She'd been very attentive the next day to make sure that her solar battery charger was always aligned to best advantage to the sun.

Something was changing inside her. Patty had come to the wilderness for her wolves and the silence of nature, but like a bear to a honey trap, she couldn't resist circling back to the fire tower atop Gray Wolf Summit.

It wasn't even the sex.

Okay. It wasn't just the sex.

When they were together, nothing else existed. There were visits when they hardly spoke a word. She would track him to his cabin atop the summit, take all he could give her, sleep in his arms, and be gone back to the wolves by daybreak. Such a heavy sleeper, he rarely woke to see her off. But when he did, he always caressed her gently and kissed her sweetly. One of those wordless nights he'd spent hours tracing every line of her wolf tattoo as if stamping its joy onto her soul more deeply than the tattoo artist had.

Other visits, they might not make love at all. Just watch the sunset, curl up in each other's arms, and sleep. They talked

of nothing and everything, but only about
the present. Neither of them had a past or
future. Neither of them even had a name.

Patty was not her mother nor was she
her grandmother or even her great-gran.
They had all married their men at sixteen or
seventeen and given birth well before the
acceptable nine months had passed.

The one thing Patty knew for certain,
being with a man for more than a time or
two was too great a risk. Too dangerous.
But again that bear to the honey trap; she
could no more resist Fireboy than he
could her.

He'd taken to doing the town food-run
for both of them so that she didn't have to
leave the wilderness. On his way down the
mountain, he would radio, gather what little
trash she couldn't burn, and bring back
an extra twenty pounds of supplies. He
never stayed away overnight, though she
never let him return directly to the tower
unrewarded.

If the wolves were running that night,
she'd sneak him into one of the blinds
she'd created along the primary trail. He'd

been nervous as hell the first couple times, even after she assured him that wolves didn't attack humans. But as they watched The Messenger through the view screen on her night-vision camera—and the female had given them little more than a sideways glance—he'd settled down. When the wolf was gone, they made love among the soft ferns with the rich smell of the forest duff wrapped around them.

"Wolfgirl!" the radio snapped at her early on a hot August afternoon.

A startled rabbit leapt and bolted from close beside Patty's position.

The Messenger shot after it, but Patty knew the wolf would be too late.

"What?" she yelled back into the radio.

"Where are you?"

"Go away!"

She began gathering her camera gear and was about to shut off the radio in frustration—the rabbit would have made a great catch and she knew how hard it was getting for the old wolf to hunt. This wouldn't be her last season, but the end had just come a little closer.

"Where are you? It's important," he shouted at her.

"Head of Long Tail Creek, about two hundred yards above the western den."

"You need to get out of there. Get up onto the ridge trail. Either get to me or get off the mountain."

"Why?" But she heard why. She found a break in the forest canopy and caught a glimpse of a black airplane painted with orange-and-red flames like a sports car. Even as she watched, small figures dressed in yellow tumbled out of the rear and then popped open parachutes.

Two smokejumpers. Four.

The plane circled back, four more.

And a third time.

Two smokejumpers is what they sent to stop a typical small fire, under an acre. Four could beat down a half dozen acres. A dozen smokies was very bad news indeed.

A helicopter came in.

Instead of delivering more smokejumpers up high, it came in so low that she had to cover her ears as it by passed overhead and continued down into the steep valley. Then there was a high whine, momentarily louder than the roaring engines and the pounding rotors, and a shower of red retardant sheeted from the sky down onto the forest in the valley far below her—but not that far.

The wind, almost undetectable down here in the trees, was brushing downslope, which would explain why she hadn't smelled any wood smoke. Even though the wind might be washing down the hill, fire loved to climb.

Patty was a dozen scrambling steps upslope before she caught herself.

The Messenger hadn't smelled the wood smoke either. And if she hadn't, then the wolves in the den down below hadn't.

It was absurd, she was human, they were wolves. But she knew them, had named and cataloged each one, knew them by their markings, their behaviors, even the half-grown pups. Of them all, only The Messenger remained nameless to her.

Another helo roared by low overhead, another sheet of red cascading from the sky.

"Wolfgirl, tell me you're on the move."

She wasn't. She was frozen between escape and saving—

Patty plunged down the slope, smashing a shoulder against a tree to slow herself down when her speed went out of control, jumping over a boulder that threatened to kneecap her and landing a dozen feet below in a roll that was only broken when she tumbled into a blackberry patch. Cursing and bleeding from a dozen scratches, she circled wide below the den.

The roar of chainsaws and heart-stopping thunder of crashing trees below told that the trouble was far closer than she'd like.

Approach the den from below.

The pack was out front, agitated by the noise, but not frightened by the fire they couldn't smell. Blackthorne the big male pacing back and forth. Mariko, the small pack's second female—Blackthorne's true love in *Shogun*—was guarding the pups, keeping them confined in the cave.

Patty climbed back toward them.

"Shoo! Move!" The massive black pack leader turned to face her but, other than a worried snarl, made no effort to move off. She didn't dare move any closer, he might attack her in simple panic. Then she had an idea.

Patty pulled out her can of bear pepper spray. She shot the smallest squirt she could upslope and a bit to the side.

She heard a sharp *Yip!* from Blackthorne just as she realized her mistake. The rising heat of the fire below them was now actively pulling air downslope to feed itself. The pepper spray she'd shot near the wolf was also dragged right back down on her.

It wafted into her face.

She cried out in pain as it hit her eyes and nostrils despite her raised arm. Diving down, she rubbed her face in the soft ferns and cool earth. She screamed out the pain that even that small amount of spray had caused.

When she could finally see again, Blackthorne was gone. The female was following and several bushy-tailed youngsters disappeared with them into the brush— upslope, thank god.

She couldn't count how many pups through her streaming eyes, so she

forced her way up to the den. A lone
twenty-pound pup had been left behind,
Vasco by his markings—one white ear,
one black—the Portuguese pilot and
Blackthorne's lone friend. So terrified that
he didn't even nip at her as she reached in
to drag him out.

Patty struggled up the steep slope.

What had been a crashing three-minute
descent became a brutal half-hour climb.
She tried releasing Vasco, dropping him
to the ground and shooing him upwards
but he merely cowered at her feet, front
paw raised. She saw it had a nasty cut and
probably hurt too much to walk on. It
would heal in the den, could be ignored
in a three-footed run across level ground,
but the pup couldn't climb a steep slope
with it.

She eventually became aware of two
things.

The rising heat wasn't only from her
hard climb, the fire was starting to run up
the narrow cleft.

The other thing was Fireboy's near
frantic calls.

"I'm headed upslope," she answered in between raged gasps. "I have an injured pup. But the fire's close. It's hot."

"God damn it, Wolfgirl. Drop it and run!"

She knew that was the smart thing, the wise thing but, "I can't," her voice came out as a sob and she kept struggling up the slope.

As she climbed past where the initial radio call had spooked the rabbit and The Messenger, she started scanning for the female. There was no question, she would know to run. Wouldn't she? Patty hadn't.

There was still no smell of smoke, just the insufferable heat.

Patty continued battling her way through the brush. The slope rose so steeply that her sore knee—she must have cracked it against something during her pell-mell descent—often banged against tree roots and rocks.

Would the wolf pup tolerate being inside a fire shelter with her? She doubted it, but they might have no choice.

That's when she noticed her pack was gone. She'd shed it somewhere. Her camera, data, and radio were attached to her fanny pack, but all of her clothes and gear were lost somewhere in the trees and boulders. And in it was the foil fire shelter kept for true, last-resort emergencies.

A glance back over her shoulder was a bad mistake. The fire had reached the den, only three hundred yards below her, but with flames reaching hundreds of feet above the hundred-foot tall trees. Even glancing over her shoulder, the heat was a slap on the face. And the roar, the roar was deafening.

There might have been a radio call, but she couldn't hear it over the fire's howl.

She turned and kept climbing though her knee throbbed at every step. The stitch in her side was so bad that she was almost weeping into the wolf pup's fur. Every step had become agony.

Bear down, soldier! There is no such thing as quitting!

She bore down, but she didn't have much to bear down with.

The roar and the wind peaked, slamming against her so hard that all she could do was drop to her knees and wait for it.

"Hi."

Patty screamed as a hand touched her on the shoulder.

A man clad in yellow Nomex and a pilot's helmet dangled at the end of a wire not a foot from her.

Patty's gaze followed the wire upward until she spotted the helicopter hovering high above the trees, its engines even louder than the fire, the downblast shaking trees and brush.

"Steve Mercer, Mount Hood Aviation. How about we get out of here?"

She held the wolf pup closer, "I'm not leaving Vasco."

The man swept the pup under one arm—Vasco whined nervously but accepted the transfer—and twisted a lifting ring toward her. It was also attached to the wire; he held it so that the opening faced Patty.

It was like a circular orange life preserver.

"Head, arms, and shoulders through the hole," he instructed as calmly as if they were on a quiet street corner. "Keep your arms down so that it catches you in the armpits. Keeping them down locks you in place."

She did as he said and moments later they were lifting up out of the trees, spinning slowly, too much like a rotisserie in the approaching fire's heat.

Once they were clear of the trees, the helo pulled them away from the fire and she could start to breathe again. A hundred feet above the trees, the flames still reached far higher, but they were rapidly falling astern as they continued to climb up the slope.

"Emily says that we'll drop you at the base of the mountain," the man shouted to her.

"Can you drop us near the top?"

10

Patty curled up on the fire tower's bunk and tended the wolf pup. Calming the young wolf let her not think about how her eyes still stung, how much her knee hurt, or quite how close she'd come to dying.

She listened as Fireboy worked the radio through the long afternoon.

The smokejumpers fought the fire in pitched battle until it was trapped and couldn't spread either way along the valley wall. The helicopters had contained it before it crossed the ridge. The second den would be safe.

If The Messenger lived, perhaps she'd guide Blackthorne's pack over to join the larger one to the east.

She buried her face in Vasco's fur and wept for only the second time since that day as a young girl when she had understood the trap that her family was in. It was the day she'd determined to find a way out.

Patty had wept that first time in Fireboy's arms as some impossible sense of loss had overwhelmed her, even if she hadn't known what the loss had been. And now she wept because she understood that from the first time with him, what she had left behind was the Warrior Girl fighting for freedom against all odds. In his powerful arms, she was more truly herself than anywhere she'd ever been.

A long time later, Fireboy sat down close beside her, but didn't touch her.

The sun had gone, but she hadn't noticed.

"Is it out?" her voice was rough and still stung from the pepper spray she'd inhaled.

"Yes," he nodded in the soft light of the small oil lamp that he'd lit. "A ground team has arrived and is making sure it stays dead. The smokies are already being lifted out by the helos. We have another fire north of Cougar Peak that they're needed on. How's the pup?"

She held up the long and sharp stone sliver that she'd extracted from Vasco's pad, "He'll heal fine now."

"Is he like a permanent addition to the family?"

"No, I can probably reintroduce him to his pack tomorrow. I think I know where they've moved to." And Patty knew she'd find The Messenger there, she just had to.

Then his words registered.

"The family?"

He shrugged easily, "Does seem to be what I said."

As she watched his face shifted. One moment he was casual, keeping up a cool façade. The next was a wash of emotion she couldn't even recognize, but both his hands were crushing down on one of hers.

"I thought I'd lost you. I've never been so afraid in my life. I couldn't imagine this world without you in it. To never be able to talk to you again, laugh with you again, it simply wasn't possible, but it felt so real. I could barely help on the fire until they found you."

"Family?" she couldn't seem to get past the word. Was family about something more than mere survival? Hers had never been.

But she could see in his eyes that she did mean the world to him. She didn't need his crushing grip nor his eyes glistening in the soft lamplight to know that he'd been afraid to the very core. For her. Of losing her.

"I've never been important to anyone," Patty told him. "Not that important."

"I swear I almost went charging down into the fire myself to find you. If that Mount Hood Aviation helo hadn't called that they had you, I would have. I never knew what was important—that anything *could be* that important to me—until I met you."

And she could see the truth of that. He really would have run right into the fire for her.

The strange thing was, she'd have done the same for him. Without knowing how it happened, she'd discovered what family was supposed to be. It wasn't about surviving together, it was about helping each other. Not just from a fire, but from the heart.

She raised her free hand—the one not still locked in his crushing grip—from the pup's fur and brushed it over his cheek. How could she describe how she felt about him? How could she explain anything to someone who made her feel so important, so precious?

She leaned forward to kiss him lightly on the lips and then leaned back to look him in the eyes.

"Patty Dale," she whispered because what could be more important than a name.

"Tom Cunningham."

She listened to her heart and knew. Knew that this was simply right. As nothing in her life had ever been, even more than wildlife biology.

"Patty Cunningham?" She asked it softly, as much of herself as of him.

His smile was all the answer she needed.

About the Author

M. L. Buchman has over 40 novels in print. His military romantic suspense books have been named Barnes & Noble and NPR "Top 5 of the year" and Booklist "Top 10 of the Year." In addition to romance, he also writes thrillers, fantasy, and science fiction.

In among his career as a corporate project manager he has: rebuilt and single-handed a fifty-foot sailboat, both flown and jumped out of airplanes, designed and built two houses, and bicycled solo around the world. He is now making his living as a full-time writer on the Oregon Coast with his beloved wife. He is constantly amazed at what you can do with a degree in Geophysics. You may keep up with his writing by subscribing to his newsletter at www.mlbuchman.com.

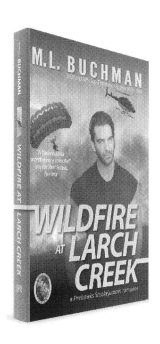

Wildfire at Larch Creek
(a Firehawks romance
excerpt)

Two-Tall Tim Harada leaned over Akbar the Great's shoulder to look out the rear door of the DC-3 airplane.

"Ugly," he shouted over the roar of the engine and wind.

Akbar nodded rather than trying to speak.

Since ugly was their day job, it didn't bother Tim much, but this was worse than usual. It would be their fourth smokejump in nine days on the same fire. The Cottonwood Peak Fire was being a total pain in the butt, even worse than usual for a wildfire. Every time they blocked it in one direction, the swirling winds would turnabout and drive the fire toward a new point on the compass. Typical for the Siskiyou Mountains of northern California, but still a pain.

Akbar tossed out a pair of crepe paper streamers and they watched together. The foot-wide streamers caught wind and curled, loop-the-looped through vortices, and reversed direction at least three times. Pretty much the worst conditions possible for a parachute jump.

"It's what we live for!"

Akbar nodded and Tim didn't have to see his best friend's face to know about the fierce wildness of his white grin on his Indian-dark face. Or the matching one against his own part-Vietnamese coloring. Many women told him that his mixed Viet, French-Canadian, and Oklahoman blood made him intriguingly exotic—a fact that had never hurt his prospects in the bar.

The two of them were the first-stick smokejumpers for Mount Hood Aviation, the best freelance firefighters of them all. This was—however moronic—*precisely* what they lived for. He'd followed Akbar the Great's lead for five years and the two of them had climbed right to the top.

"Race you," Akbar shouted then got on the radio and called directions about the best line of attack to "DC"—who earned his nickname from his initials matching the DC-3 jump plane he piloted.

Tim moved to give the deployment plan to the other five sticks still waiting on their seats; no need to double check it with Akbar, the best approach was obvious. Heck, this was the top crew. The other smokies barely needed the briefing; they'd all been watching through their windows as the streamers cavorted in the chaotic winds.

Then, while DC turned to pass back over the jump zone, he and Akbar checked each others' gear. Hard hat with heavy mesh face shield, Nomex fire suit tight at the throat, cinched at the waist, and tucked in the boots. Parachute and reserve properly buckled, with the static line clipped to the wire above the DC-3's jump door. Pulaski fire axe, fire shelter, personal gear bag, chain saw on a long rope tether, gas can…the list went on, and through long practice took them under ten seconds to verify.

Five years they'd been jumping together, the last two as lead stick. Tim's body ached, his head swam with fatigue, and he was already hungry though they'd just eaten a full meal at base camp and a couple energy bars on the short flight back to the fire. All the symptoms were typical for a long fire.

DC called them on close approach. Once more Akbar leaned out the door, staying low enough for Tim to lean out over him. Not too tough as Akbar was a total shrimp and Tim had earned the "Two-Tall" nickname for being two Akbars tall.

He wasn't called Akbar the Great for his height, but rather for his powerful build and unstoppable energy on the fire line.

"Let's get it done and…" Tim shouted in Akbar's ear as they approached the jump point.

"…come home to Mama!" and Akbar was gone.

Tim actually hesitated before launching himself after Akbar and ended up a hundred yards behind him.

Come home to Mama? Akbar had always finished the line, *Go get the girls.* Ever since the wedding, Akbar had gotten all weird in the head. Just because he was married and happy was no excuse to—

The static line yanked his chute. He dropped below the tail of the DC-3— always felt as if he had to duck, but doorways on the ground did the same thing to him—and the chute caught air and jerked him hard in the groin.

The smoke washed across the sky. High, thin cirrus clouds promised an incoming weather change, but wasn't going to help them much today. The sun was still pounding the wilderness below with a scorching, desiccating heat that turned trees into firebrands at a single spark.

The Cottonwood Peak Fire was chewing across some hellacious terrain. Hillsides so steep that some places you needed mountaineering gear to go chase the flames. Hundred-and-fifty foot Doug firs popping off like fireworks. Ninety-six thousand acres, seventy percent contained and a fire as angry as could be that they were beating it down.

Tim yanked on the parachute's control lines as the winds caught him and tried to fling him back upward into the sky. On a jump like this you spent as much time making sure that the chute didn't tangle with itself in the chaotic winds as you did trying to land somewhere reasonable.

Akbar had called it right though. They had to hit high on this ridge and hold it. If not, that uncontained thirty percent of the wildfire was going to light up a whole new valley to the east and the residents of Hornbrook, California were going to have a really bad day.

His chute spun him around to face west toward the heart of the blaze. Whoever had rated this as seventy per-cent contained clearly needed his head examined. Whole hillsides were still alight with flame. It was only because the MHA smokies had cut so many firebreaks over the last eight days, combined with the constant pounding of the big Firehawk helicopters dumping retardant loads every which way, that the whole mountain range wasn't on fire.

Tim spotted Akbar. Below and to the north. Damn but that guy could fly a chute. Tim dove hard after him.

Come home to Mama! Yeesh! But the dog had also found the perfect lady. Laura Jenson: wilderness guide, expert horse-woman—who was still trying to get Tim up on one of her beasts—and who was really good for Akbar. But it was as if Tim no longer recognized his best friend.

They used to crawl out of a fire, sack out in the bunks for sixteen-straight, then go hit the bars. *What do I do for a living? I parachute out of airplanes to fight wildfires by hand.* It wowed the women every time, gained them pick of the crop.

Now when Akbar hit the ground, Laura would be waiting in her truck and they'd disappear to her little cabin in the woods. What was up with that anyway?

Tim looked down and cursed. He should have been paying more attention. Akbar was headed right into the center of the only decent clearing, and Tim was on the verge of overflying the ridge and landing in the next county.

He yanked hard on the right control of his chute, swung in a wide arc, and prayed that the wind gods would be favorable just this once. They were, by inches. Instead of smacking face first into the drooping top of a hemlock that he hadn't seen coming, he swirled around it, receiving only a breath-stealing slap to the ribs, and dropped in close beside Akbar.

"Akbar the Great rules!"

His friend demanded a high five for making a cleaner landing than Tim's before he began stuffing away his chute.

In two minutes, the chutes were in their stuff bags and they'd shifted over to fire-fighting mode. The next two sticks dropped into the space they'd just vacated. Krista nailed her landing more cleanly than Tim or Akbar had. Jackson ate an aspen, but it was only a little one, so he was on the ground just fine, but he had to cut down the tree to recover his chute. Didn't matter; they had to clear the whole ridge anyway—except everyone now had an excuse to tease him.

# # #

Forty hours later Tim had spent thirty hours non-stop on the line and ten crashed face first into his bunk. Those first thirty had been a grueling battle of clearing the ridgeline and scraping the earth down to mineral soils. The heat had been obscene as the fire climbed the face of the ridge, rising until it had towered over them in a wall of raging orange and thick, smoke-swirl black a couple dozen stories high.

The glossy black-and-racing-flame painted dots of the MHA Firehawks had looked insignificant as they dove, dropping eight tons of bright-red retardant alongside the fire or a thousand gallons of water directly on the flames as called for. The smaller MD500s were on near-continuous call-up to douse hotspots where sparks had jumped the line. Emily, Jeannie, and Vern, their three night-drop certified pilots, had flown right through the night to help them kill it. Mickey and the others picking it back up at daybreak.

Twice they'd been within minutes of having to run and once they were within seconds of deploying their fire shelters, but they'd managed to beat it back each time. There was a reason that smokejumpers were called on a Type I wildfire incident. They delivered. And the Mount Hood Aviation smokies had a reputation of being the best in the business; they'd delivered on that as well.

Tim had hammered face down into his bunk, too damn exhausted to shower first. Which meant his sheets were now char-smeared and he'd have to do a load of laundry. He jumped down out of the top bunk, shifting sideways to not land on Akbar if he swung out of the lower bunk at the same moment…except he wasn't there. His sheets were neat and clean, the blanket tucked in. Tim's were the only set of boots on the tiny bit of floor the two of them usually jostled for. Akbar now stayed overnight in the bunkhouse only if Laura was out on a wilderness tour ride with her horses.

Tim thought about swapping his sheets for Akbar's clean ones, but it hardly seemed worth the effort.

Following tradition, Tim went down the hall, kicking the doors and receiving back curses from the crashed-out smokies. The MHA base camp had been a summer camp for Boy Scouts or something way too many years ago. The halls were narrow and the doors thin.

"Doghouse!" he hollered as he went. He raised a fist to pound on Krista's door when a voice shouted from behind it.

"You do that, Harada, and I'm gonna squish your tall ass down to Akbar's runt size."

That was of course a challenge and he beat on her door with a quick rattle of both fists before sprinting for the safety of the men's showers.

Relative safety.

He was all soaped up in the doorless plywood shower stall, when a bucket of ice-cold water blasted him back against the wall.

He yelped! He couldn't help himself. She must have dipped it from the glacier-fed stream that ran behind the camp it was so freaking cold.

Her raucous laugh said that maybe she had.

He considered that turnabout might be fair play, but with Krista you never knew. If he hooked up a one-and-a-half inch fire hose, she might get even with a three hundred-gallon helicopter drop. And then… Maybe he'd just shame her into buying the first round at the Doghouse Inn.

Tim resoaped and scrubbed and knew he'd still missed some patches of black. The steel sheets attached to the wall as mirrors were as useless now as they'd been before decades of Boy Scouts had tried to carve their initials into them. Usually he and Akbar checked each other because you ended up with smoke or char stains in the strangest spots.

But Akbar wasn't here.

Tim didn't dare wait for any of the others. If he was caught still in the shower by all the folks he'd just rousted from their sacks, it wouldn't turn out well.

He made it back to his room in one piece. The guys who'd showered last night were already on their way out. Good, they'd grab the table before he got down into town and hit the Doghouse Inn. The grimy ones weren't moving very fast yet.

Tim had slept through breakfast and after the extreme workout of a long fire his stomach was being pretty grouchy about that.

# # #

As Macy Tyler prepared for it, she regretted saying yes to a date with Brett Harrison. She regretted not breaking the date the second after she'd made it. And she hoped that by the time the evening with Brett Harrison was over she wouldn't regret not dying of some exotic Peruvian parrot flu earlier in the day.

Just because they'd both lived in Larch Creek, Alaska their entire lives was not reason enough for her to totally come apart. Was it?

Actually it was nothing against Brett particularly. But she knew she was still borderline psychotic about men. It was her first date since punching out her fiancé on the altar, and the intervening six months had not been sufficient for her to be completely rational on the subject.

After fussing for fifteen minutes, she gave herself up as a lost cause. Macy hanked her dark, dead straight, can't-do-crap-with-it hair back in a long ponytail, put on a bra just because—it was mostly optional with her build, and pulled on a t-shirt. Headed for the door, she caught sight of herself in the hall mirror and saw which t-shirt she'd grabbed: *Helicopter Pilots Get It Up Faster.*

She raced back to her bedroom and switched it out for: *People Fly Airplanes, Pilots Fly Helicopters.* And knocked apart her ponytail in the process. Hearing Brett's pickup on the gravel street, she left her hair down, grabbed a denim jacket, and headed for the door.

Macy hurried out and didn't give Brett time to climb down and open the door of his rattletrap Ford truck for her, if he'd even thought of it.

"Look nice, Macy," was all the greeting he managed which made her feel a little better about the state of her own nerves.

He drove into town, which was actually a bit ridiculous, but he'd insisted he would pick her up. Town was four blocks long and she only lived six blocks from the center of it. They rolled down Buck Street, up Spitz Lane, and down Dave Court to Jack London Avenue—which had the grandest name but was only two blocks long because of a washout at one end and the back of the pharmacy-gas station at the other.

This north side of town was simply "The Call" because all of the streets were named for characters from The Call of the Wild. French Pete and Jack London had sailed the Alaskan seaways together.

So, as streets were added, the founders had made sure they were named after various of London's books. Those who lived in "The Fang" to the south were stuck with characters from White Fang for their addresses including: Grey Beaver Boulevard, Weedon Way, and Lip-lip Lane.

Macy wished that she and French Pete's mate Hilma—he went on to marry an Englishwoman long after he'd left and probably forgotten Larch Creek—hadn't been separated by a century of time; the woman must have really been something.

Macy tried to start a conversation with Brett, but rapidly discovered that she'd forgotten to bring her brain along on this date and couldn't think of a thing to say.

They hit the main street at the foot of Hal's Folly—the street was only the length of the gas station, named for the idiot who drove a dogsled over thin ice and died for it in London's book. It was pure irony that the street was short and steep. When it was icy, the Folly could send you shooting across the town's main street and off into

Larch Creek—which was much more of a river than a creek. The street froze in early October, but the river was active enough that you didn't want to go skidding out onto the ice before mid-November.

Brett drove them up past the contradictory storefronts which were all on the "high side" of the road—the "low side" and occasionally the road itself disappeared for a time during the spring floods. The problem was that almost all of the buildings were from the turn of the century, but half were from the turn of this century and half were from the turn before. The town had languished during the 1900s and only experienced a rebirth over the last four decades.

Old log cabins and modern stick-framed buildings with generous windows stood side by side. Mason's Galleria was an ultra-modern building of oddly-shaded glass and no right angles. One of the town mysteries was how Mason kept the art gallery in business when Larch Creek attracted so few tourists. Macy's favorite suggestion was that the woman—who was always dressed in the sharpest New York clothes and spoke so fast that no one could understand her— was actually a front for the Alaskan mafia come to rule Larch Creek.

This newest, most modern building in town was tight beside the oldest and darkest structure.

French Pete's, where Brett parked his truck, was the anchor at the center of town and glowered out at all of the other structures. The heavy-log, two-story building dominated Parisian Way—as the main street of Larch Creek was named by the crazy French prospector who founded the town in the late-1800s. He'd named the trading post after himself and the town after the distinctive trees that painted the surrounding hills yellow every fall. French Pete had moved on, but a Tlingit woman he'd brought with him stayed and bore him a son after his departure. It was Hilma who had made sure the town thrived.

There had been a recent upstart movement to rename the town because having the town of Larch Creek *on* Larch Creek kept confusing things. "Rive

Gauche" was the current favorite during heavy drinking at French Pete's because the town was on the "left bank" of Larch Creek. If you were driving in on the only road, the whole town was on the left bank; like the heart of Paris. The change had never made it past the drinking stage, so most folk just ignored the whole topic, but it persisted on late Saturday nights.

Macy took strength from the town. She had loved it since her first memories. And just because she'd been dumb enough to agree to a date with Brett, she wasn't going to blame Larch Creek for that.

Well, not much. Perhaps, if there were more than five hundred folk this side of Liga Pass, there would be a single man that she could date who didn't know every detail of her life. She still clung onto the idea that she'd find a decent man somewhere among the chaff.

Dreamer!

That wasn't entirely fair. After all, some of them, like Brett, were decent enough.

The problem was that she, in turn, knew every detail of their lives. Macy had gone

to school with each of them for too many
years and knew them all too well. A lot
of her classmates left at a dead run after
graduation and were now up in Fairbanks,
though very few went further afield. The
thirty-mile trip back to Larch Creek from
"the city" might as well be three hundred
for how often they visited. The first half
of the trip was on Interstate 4 which was
kept open year round. But once you left
the main highway, the road narrowed and
twisted ten miles over Liga Pass with harsh
hairpins and little forgiveness. It didn't help
that it was closed as often as it was open in
the winter months. The last five miles were
through the valley's broad bottom land.

The town was four blocks long from the
Unitarian church, which was still a movie
theater on Friday and Saturday nights, at
the north end of town to the grange at
the south end. The houses crawled up the
hills to the east. And the west side of the
fast-running, glacier-fed river, where the
forested hills rose in an abrupt escarpment,
belonged to bear, elk, and wolf. Only Old
Man Parker had a place on that side, unable

to cross during fall freeze-up or spring melt-out. But he and his girlfriend didn't come into town much even when the way was open across running water or thick ice.

The main road ran north to meet the highway to Fairbanks, and in the other direction ended five miles south at Tena. Tena simply meant "trail" in the Tanana dialect and added another couple dozen families to the area. The foot trail out of Tena lead straight toward the massif of Denali's twenty-thousand foot peak which made the valley into a picture postcard.

Macy did her best to draw strength from the valley and mountain during the short drive to French Pete's. Once they hit Parisian Way, a bit of her brain returned. She even managed a polite inquiry about Brett's construction business and was pretty pleased at having done so. Thankfully they were close, so his answer was kept brief.

"Mostly it's about shoring up people's homes before winter hits. There are only a couple new homes a year and Danny gets most of those." He sounded bitter, it was a rivalry that went back to the senior prom and Cheryl Dahl, the prettiest Tanana girl in town.

The fact that Brett and Danny drank together most Saturdays and Cheryl had married Mike Nichol—the one she'd accompanied to the prom—and had three equally beautiful children in Anchorage had done nothing to ease their epic rivalry.

Or perhaps it was because Brett's blue pickup had a bumper sticker that said *America Is Under Construction* and Danny's blue truck had a drawing of his blue bulldozer that read *Vogon Constructor Fleet— specialist in BIG jobs.*

"Small towns," Macy said in the best sympathetic tone she could muster. It was difficult to not laugh in his face, because it was *so* small-town of them.

"This place looks wackier every time," they'd stopped in front of French Pete's. "Carl has definitely changed something, just can't pick it out."

Macy looked up in surprise. The combined bar and restaurant appeared no different to her. Big dark logs made a structure two-stories high with a steep roof to shed the snow. A half dozen broad steps led up to a deep porch that had no room for humans; it was jammed with Carl Deville's collection of "stuff."

"Your junk. My stuff," Carl would always say when teased about it by some unwary tourist. After such an unthinking comment, they were then as likely to find horseradish in their turkey sandwich as not.

There was the broken Iditarod sled from Vic Hornbeck's failed race bid in the late 1970s piled high with dropped elk antlers. An Elks Lodge hat from Poughkeepsie, New York still hung over one handle of the sled. The vintage motorcycle of the guy who had come through on his way to solo climb up Denali from the north along Muldrow Glacier and descend to the south by Cassin Ridge was still there, buried under eleven years of detritus. Whether he made the crossing and didn't come back or died on the mountain, no one ever knew.

"Man asked me to hold it for him a bit," Carl would offer in his deep laconic style when asked by some local teen who lusted after the wheels. "Don't see no need to hustle it out from under him. 'Sides, the baby girl he left in Carol Swenson's belly whilst he was here is ten now. Mayhaps she'll want it at sixteen."

There was an old wooden lobster pot— that Macy had never understood because the Gulf of Alaska to the south wasn't all that much closer than the Beaufort Sea to the north and the pot looked like it was from Maine—with a garden gnome-sized bare-breasted hula dancer standing inside it; her ceramic paint worn to a patina by too many Alaskan winters spent topless and out of doors. A hundred other objects were scattered about including worn-out gold panning equipment, a couple of plastic river kayaks with "For Rent" signs that might have once been green and sky blue before the sun leached out all color— though she'd never seen them move. And propped in the corner was the wooden propeller from Macy's first plane that she'd snapped when her wheel had caught in an early hole in the permafrost up near Nenana. That was before she'd switched to helicopters. She'd spent a week there before someone could fly in a replacement.

"Looks the same to me."

Brett eyed her strangely as he held open the door.

And just like that she knew she'd blown what little hope this date had right out of the water. Brett had been trying to make conversation and she'd done her true-false test. It wasn't like she was anal, it was more like everyone simply treated her as if she was.

Inside was dark, warm, and just as cluttered. A century or more of oddbits had been tacked to the walls: old photos, snowshoes strung with elk hide, a rusted circular blade several feet across from the old sawmill that had closed back in the sixties, and endless other bits and pieces that Carl and his predecessors had gathered. He claimed direct lineage back to French Pete Deville, through Hilma. It wasn't hard to believe; Carl looked like he'd been born behind the bar. Looked like he might die there too.

The fiction section of the town library lined one long wall of French Pete's. Most of the non-fiction was down at the general store except for religion, movies, and anything to do with mechanics. They were down in the movie house-church's lobby, the mechanical guides because the pharmacy-gas station was next door.

Though Carl didn't have any kin, Natalie, the ten-year-old daughter of Carol Swenson and the mountain climber with the left-behind motorcycle, was sitting up on a high barstool playing chess against Carl. It was a place she could be found most days when there wasn't school and Carol was busy over at the general store and post office. She was such a fixture that over the last few years everyone had pretty much come to expect Natty to take over French Pete's someday.

Macy scanned the tables hoping that no one would recognize her, fat chance in a community the size of Larch Creek.

And then she spotted the big table back in the corner beneath the moose-antler chandelier. It was packed.

Oh crap!

She'd forgotten it was Sunday.

Too late to run for cover, she guided Brett in the other direction to a table in the corner. She managed to sit with her back to her father's expression of mock horror. That she could deal with.

But it would have been easier if Mom hadn't offered a smile and a wink.

Available at fine retailers everywhere

More information at:
www.mlbuchman.com

.

20637712R00063

Printed in Great Britain
by Amazon